Delton

Benjamin Fun

Suited Word

Books in the series

Delton Guardians

Gravelburn's Revenge

The Espinox Trials

Delton Guardians

Contents

Chapter One
Surprise Attack

They had horned helmets and spiked shoulder plates.
Unusually, they had marched the last few hours in half-steps,
and without the singing and war chants. But that had all
been part of the plan. Under the cover of darkness, they
stealthily advanced on their target.

Without turning around, Gravelburn gently tapped the arm of
the Rochgwar behind him. The Rochgwar silently passed on
the signal to those around him, and they passed it down their
lines. They had reached the edge of the forest, and the trees
would not offer them any more cover. They were at what
training manuals called the FEBA – forward edge of battle
area. And all that stood between them and their enemies
was open ground. Now it was time to rest and wait.

Gravelburn allowed himself a smirk. Everything so far had been so ... so ... what was the word? He could not think of anything other than 'different'. Their enemies would be in for one big surprise. They expected Rochgwars to march to battles while singing their war songs, giving away their position long before they arrived. Even the ground trembled a warning under their usual stomping march, allowing time for enemy defences to be prepared. Their enemies expected Rochgwar attacks at dusk, just before light was fading, because as the battle progressed, the darkening sky gave Rochgwars the advantage – they were more used to darker surroundings. But this attack would be ... different. Gravelburn was one step ahead.

*   *   *

Inside the base

The junior Guardians were roused from sleep earlier than usual that morning. There was more work to be done. Routine tasks had added up over the past week after some

8

of the senior Guardians had left to seek help from the other bases. The juniors had to take on some of the responsibilities of those who were not around.

Fil (pronounced 'File') stifled a yawn. He had a day of chopping wood, weapon maintenance and some training to look forward to. Each day he had to sharpen a few more wooden javelins and arrow heads, until the seniors got back. He hoped that they would return soon with food supplies, which meant every one could go back to full bowls of soup, bigger portions of bread and meaty delights instead of rationing. How he hated rationing! *The seniors can maintain their own weapons too,* he thought. *Instead of leaving it for us juniors to do!*

*   *   *

Outside the base

Gravelburn bided his time. He watched the foot patrol circle around the perimeter, their torches easily giving away their

9

current positions. He had timed them on their last few rounds, and observed that they took about one hundred counts to go around the perimeter. He noted the sentries in their watchtowers. Even though it was still dark, he and his men were careful not to make any sound that might draw attention.

He had never carried out a dawn attack before. But he was not going into it blind. Someone had tipped him off about the guard routine. There were four sentries all the time, one at each watchtower. But his enemies only sent out foot patrols at night, to walk around the perimeter. Usually there were two patrols, but this had been recently reduced to one because there were fewer people around. And just before dawn, the first day sentries would replace the last night sentries at the watchtowers. The night sentries would then climb down and briefly open the gates of the base to bring in the foot patrols. *That will be the time*, Gravelburn had decided. *That will be the time.*

10

Chapter Two
Not Just Another Day

Inside the base

The junior Guardians slept in shared bunks on beds made from logs, and lined with blankets and fur. Ember preferred just the logs. He didn't think the linings made any difference and had given his to Cut. Cut must have thought the extra padding was heavenly. He was always the last to rise.

'Time to get up, Cut! I spy something beginning with 'F'!' shouted Nitro.

'What is it?' asked Heath, always game for a laugh, egging Nitro on.

'Floor!' exclaimed Nitro, as he lifted one side of Cut's bed and slid the sleepy Guardian onto the ground.

11

'Just give it a rest, will you?' complained Cut, rubbing his head. 'You and your silly games!'

'I spy with my little eye, something beginning with –' Nitro dragged out the ending. 'O!'

'It'll be "ouch!" when I'm finished with you,' Cut muttered, moving angrily towards Nitro.

'Break it up, guys!' said Robin. The others moved in to separate Cut and Nitro. There was a commotion as Cut sought revenge, and Nitro kept dodging out of his way, infuriating him further. Cut picked up anything he could see, even if it didn't belong to him, and hurled it at Nitro, annoying the owners of the items. Junior Guardians from the other rooms came to see what was going on and soon there were chants of 'fight, fight, fight' and chaotic scenes. Early in the morning.

*   *   *

Outside the base

Gravelburn watched the foot patrol like a hawk observes its prey. As he saw the patrol disappear around the corner, he silently advanced a small team of his warriors. The six of them crawled towards the gate, moving a little at a time, every Rochgwar taking his cue from their leader. If he stopped, they did too. But the trailing Rochgwars didn't really need to watch Gravelburn to see what they had to do. They themselves could see the torch when the sentries reappeared around the corner, and that was good enough an indication to stop for the moment. And as long as the Rochgwars stayed still and made little sound when the foot patrol neared, that was fine. The darkness hid them from the sentries. Slowly and silently, they covered the open ground to the base without arousing attention.

*   *   *

Inside the base

'Junior Guardians! May I remind you that you are no longer infants, and as such, that kind of behaviour is not acceptable!' Murx Espin sternly addressed the group of children. 'In the absence of some of the senior Guardians, there is even more of a need for you to be a good example for the infants!'

The children stood rooted in an area strewn with their possessions. They all looked to the ground. No one dared to lift his eyes. They usually didn't have much contact with Murx Espin. The commanding officer was usually in a different part of the base, but he was now involved in their training, because they were short of manpower.

'I have not had any word from the Guardians that left last week, but I cannot think that they will be long now. And what will they say about you, when they come back and see you squabbling amongst yourselves?'

14

Not a word was spoken. No one dared raise his eyes.
Murx Espin looked them over. In the silence that followed, he
seemed to have regained his calm. To the junior Guardians,
he now seemed more of an elderly beloved grandad, rather
than a short-tempered general. The anger in his voice also
seemed to have gone away as he addressed them again.

'Tidy up your quarters. Get yourself ready for breakfast. Let's
start training after that. Make sure you have your weapons
with you. I'll see you outside the medical hut at the third horn
call. Any questions?'

'Rochgwar!' a shout rang out.

Chapter Three
Foiled

Gravelburn and his five Rochgwars had made it to the gates without being seen. Two Rochgwars had positioned themselves at either side of each gate, and when the gates were opened, the Guardians were surprised and overpowered. The Rochgwar team now had control and firmly held the gates open, ready for the rest of the army to push through.

'Graagh!' ('Attack!')

This was the word the Rochgwars had been waiting to hear. They let loose with their war cries, and the ground shook with their thunderous footsteps as rows of Rochgwars rushed forward to attack.

Inside Delton, Guardians – seniors and juniors – fought them off with swords and other makeshift weapons.

The Rochgwars sniggered with evil delight as they repeatedly pushed back the lines of Guardians. Children? They were easily outnumbered and dispossessed of their weapons. And the adults? The Rochgwars had them pinned back with no place to hide.

Suddenly, more Guardians rushed in through the gates! Where had they come from? They were the ones that were returning from a week ago, and the timing could not have been better! Gravelburn turned around in surprise to see scores of Guardians now attacking the back row of his army, steadily picking his men off and moving forward towards him. The Guardians he had pinned back moments ago now also surged forward. Moments ago his voice was cackling with laughter. Now it was cracking – with anger! The Rochgwars had been on the verge of victory. Now they found themselves sandwiched between two groups of Guardians!

They had advanced themselves into a losing position! How could that have happened?

The excitement that the Rochgwars felt quickly turned to panic. They swung wildly around at anyone. The discipline they had showed earlier completely evaporated and Gravelburn and his men had no choice but to retreat. They were losing numbers rapidly. They had to fight their way out of a base they had only just breached. It could not get any sillier than that. *'Grigha ga grana!'* cursed Gravelburn in Old Rochgwarian. ('Those stupid Guardians!')

Flailing wildly, the Rochgwars fought their way out before they were trapped, and retreated to the forest. Their footsteps faded as they fell back, but the anger they felt did not. *'Grai grud grun!'* shouted Grunted, Gravelburn's second-in-command. (It means, 'You'll pay for this!')

The Guardians regrouped. The wounded were helped away to be treated. In the middle of the Guardians, a small eight-year-old was still trembling with fear. Jack was an orphan and had brown hair. It was all in a mess now after the fierce fighting. He wiped the sweat off his brow. Strangely it looked red – he then realised it was blood! His heart raced.

*   *   *

A few hours later, back in the Rochgwar camp, Gravelburn was not happy. *'Epso geghrax!'* he cursed.

Gravelburn rarely used Old Rochgwarian. It was only spoken when he needed to insult or when he was angry. And at this point in time, there was someone he was particularly furious with – Grunted.

They had talked it over before they left the camp. 'Small team infiltrate. Main body attack. Reserve force defend the gate.' Gravelburn had listed out his plan to Grunted, asking him if he understood it, and the latter had nodded vigorously.

Grunted had been ordered to spread his Rochgwars out to stop any outside help from arriving while Gravelburn's other Rochgwars were attacking within. But when the battle was raging, he could not help but join in the noise and excitement inside Delton. And so he had thought *'Grig griet Grabulbun!'* ('I will just go and help Gravelburn'), taken his men in to join the battle, leaving his position undefended and allowing the Guardians to be reinforced.

At the parade the next day, Gravelburn called Grunted out. Grunted marched out from his place to the front of the parade. He saluted Gravelburn and waited for the salute to be acknowledged before he dropped his arm. But instead Gravelburn dropped him to the floor with a punch so forceful, the 'T*hwack!*' could be heard ten rows down the ranks.

It was a surprise that Grunted didn't crumble under the force of the blow. Stunned, he recovered slowly, but before he could fully get to his feet, Gravelburn informed the troops

20

that Grunted would be demoted to the rank of captain and a Flygwar named Gargna would soon be taking his place.

The Flygwars were the distant cousins of Rochgwars. Physically, they were alike, except that Flygwars had wings and could fly four feet off the ground, giving them an advantage in battle. And a whole tribe of Flygwars was on the way now to reinforce the Rochgwar army. To wreak even more havoc on the Delton Guardians.

Chapter Four
Sleepless

The damage from the battle was extensive, but most of the repair work was nearly finished. It helped that there were Guardians from other bases now with them, even if this was only for the time being, before they returned to their own. There were more people to help with security and maintenance. They had also brought more food supplies, which was a relief to those who had been through two weeks of rationing. In a way, Robin thought, even though the base was still recovering from the Rochgwar attack, life in the past five days was better than it had been for a while. Lying in his bed, he cast his eyes at the thin slice of moon that lit the sky. What was life really like outside the base? Would there be a time when the fighting would end? Would his life simply be fighting after fighting? What would his parents have thought?

It wasn't Cut's snoring that was keeping him up that night, but these thoughts that kept running through his head. At least Heath's bed was empty – he was shadowing at the watchtower that night. Junior Guardians occasionally 'shadowed' their seniors, following them around as they carried out their duties, so they could see what they had to do in the years to come.

Heath was always telling jokes after lights out and keeping everyone awake. Once he had waited until everyone was asleep before he got up to switch their boots around, watching in amusement in the morning when everyone else had mismatched boots. Even though the junior Guardians were angry, they had to shield Heath from Fil, who had been so furious that he was throwing the wrong boots and every other boot he could find in the bunk at Heath. Heath, of course, was just beside himself, watching Fil go crazy, and the other Guardians he had just pranked protecting him from a raging lunatic. And to top it all off, one of the seniors, Lex Cerberus, had arrived at the scene of the early morning

23

commotion to find Fil in that rampaging mood, and assigned him to three days of cleaning toilets! Of course, during that time, Heath had always made sure to drink lots of water. Robin thought that even Heath would be struggling to stay positive on a night like this. The cold wind howled ferociously. The watchtowers had an open wall to allow for a clear view, and Heath might just be in the one that faced the bitter wind.

Strong winds and other kinds of bad weather of course provided good cover for Flygwars. They didn't fly high enough to be affected by winds like birds do, but being able to hover over the ground gave them an advantage in speed over their cousins. They couldn't come through the forest trail that the Rochgwars frequently used, because they would have just been slowed down by branches. So they had to go around the edge of the forest, out in the open. Bad weather and visibility meant they could stay undetected. And they moved fast. When one Rochgwar had whined that the Flygwars could move out of the base after him, and still arrive at the objective before him, Gargna had wickedly mocked, *'Evolvas! Evolvas!'* ('Evolve! Evolve!')

Gargna had now arrived at the link-up point. The Flygwars were having a rest in the shadows. All they had to do was to wait until the main force of Rochgwars arrived.

Chapter Five
Mistakes (part I)

As he laced his boots on, Robin was certain that bringing a hot drink to sentries would not be a punishable offence if he was noticed moving within the camp after lights out. Surely Heath and his mentor would not mind something to drink so they could perform better at their duties? That was good reason enough, he decided. He found a flask with some tea left over from the day inside. He sipped it and paused briefly to consider. It would pass for warm.

The last fifty yards to the watchtower were out in the open, and Robin had to dash quickly to the foot of the steps to avoid being soaked by the rain that was now starting to fall.

'Who goes there!' the adult swivelled his head around and challenged.

'It's Robin,' he answered.

'Hey Robin!' Heath answered for him. 'What are you doing here?' Robin waved the flask in his hand.

'Whoa! Thanks! I was getting a bit thirsty here. It does get a bit hard to concentrate for long, and I was just waiting to get relieved so I could go back to my nice bed and …'

'Stay alert, Heath. Return to your task. Do not leave your position,' the adult cautioned. *It sounds like Hinx Matr*, Robin thought.

'My friend's come all this way to bring us something,' Heath explained. 'Throw it up, Robin! Throw it up!'

'Shhh!' the adult hissed.

Heath ignored him. 'Go on, Robin, hard as you can. I'll catch it!'

Robin estimated the force he needed to throw the flask to the watchtower twenty feet up. He was the best at Pinpoint, one of the training exercises the junior Guardians practised, which involved hurling rocks at a target fifty feet away. He regularly attained the top grade of 'Marksman'. He aimed the flask for Heath's outstretched hands and hurled it.

Sentries don't just use their eyes. They are also trained to use other senses like sound and smell. For example, a breaking twig can give away someone's unseen position. The smell of cooked food, carried in the right direction by the wind, betrays your presence long before you arrive. Hinx Matr was also an experienced sniper. His eyes were straight ahead, looking over the open ground, but he listened to and kept up with the conversation going on behind him. And when he didn't hear the *'Thup'* of metal against palm, he instantly knew what had happened without having to turn around.

'Whoops,' said Heath as he watched the flask sail over the perimeter wall.

Chapter Six
Mistakes (part II)

Gravelburn decided this would be a good test of Gargna's abilities. The main force he led had now linked up with the Flygwars. It was time to move on to the next phase of the attack, and to see if Gargna made a better deputy than Grunted.

It was nearly two in the morning now, what the Rochgwars called dark night. Gargna motioned for two of his men to follow him, and they made their way undetected to the perimeter walls of the enemy base. Like the last time, Gravelburn had been tipped off that in bad weather like this, foot patrols were not sent out, because it was not safe for them. In any case, they could not see much. So Gravelburn did not expect that Gargna would meet any resistance.

Gargna leaned against the perimeter wall to avoid being seen. He could hear the sentries in the watchtower above talking, and thanked his lucky stars that he had avoided being spotted. He carefully checked the trip flares in each hand. Each was secured to a small branch. After his Flygwars had control of the gates, he would plant a flare by each gate and pull out the safety rings. After two seconds of delay, the flares would ignite and burn brightly, showing the advancing Rochgwars where to charge between.

Gargna started to half-loosen the safety rings in preparation. Now all he had to do was to send the two Flygwars over the walls and unlock the gates from the inside.

Gargna had just finished loosening the second safety ring when he heard a 'clunk' and something metallic landed near him. His heart raced. Was it a timed explosive? He heard the sentries talking above him, before they suddenly went quiet. Had the Flygwars been spotted? Gargna froze, and had to summon every ounce of his body to keep still, even though

31

his wings felt so tense they were ready to flap like crazy. He waited for a minute, but the metallic object did not detonate. It had landed near the base entrance. Could it be a Claymore mine, ready to explode, to ambush the Rochgwars when they advanced? Gargna could not shrug off the ominous feeling, and he needed to ensure the Rochgwars were not walking into a trap. He indicated to the men to adopt an all-round defence, which they did. Still holding his flares in his hands, and keeping close to the ground, Gargna slowly inched forward to examine the metallic object, taking care to avoid the watchful eye of the sentry above.

He was about halfway to it when the gates to the base opened and two figures walked out. Flat on his belly, clutching two flares and without his weapon in his hand, Gargna could not have felt more vulnerable. One of the figures shot out an arm. 'There!' pointed out Heath. 'I see it!'

Heath meant the flask. Gargna thought Heath was referring to him. In a brief moment of panic, he pulled the safety rings.

Chapter Seven
The Second Attack

There was a fizz as the flares sparkled to life. Momentarily
blinded, Gargna tossed them to the wet ground, but he was
fortunate that they had ignited sufficiently to burn. Overcome
by the brightness, and by the situation, Robin and Heath
also froze momentarily, but recovered enough to retreat and
sound the alarm. There would be no time to close the gates.
Gargna's Flygwars had already positioned themselves to
hold them open.

'Rochgwar attack! Enemy attack! Rochgwars!' alerted the
sentries. Robin and Heath also ran back to the sleeping
quarters, yelling at the top of their voices, banging doors to
wake the Guardians.

Hinx Matr fired from his sentry position. From the other
watchtower, Lex Cerberus did the same. The Flygwars were

supposed to have been undetected, but now they were being met with resistance, and the change in plan caused enough panic among them and gave the Guardians a few precious minutes to respond.

Even though he was still coming under fire from the sentries, Gargna judged that the Rochgwars should attack now. *'Fleesh furn nash rug!'* he roared to the darkness behind him.

The senior Guardians in the base had scrambled to respond to the alarm. Some of Robin's friends were dazed and looked angry to have been woken up, but when they heard the cry of 'Rochgwar' they sprang from their beds and the look on their faces turned from anger to worry. Each person grabbed his weapons and ran to alert others, and soon a whole base of Guardians were headed for the gates.

Where they found Gravelburn and his men all ready and waiting for them.

'Grock grag groo, Gargna,' said Gravelburn to Gargna. ('Well, well, well, good, Gargna.')

Gravelburn turned to face his enemies. The Guardians, now trapped inside their own base, raised their weapons and prepared themselves for the battle of their lives. It was a tense stand-off.

Suddenly, a flaming arrow flew through the air and broke the silence. *'Awrrr!'* came a cry from behind Gravelburn. Gravelburn was incensed.

'Gruuuuu!' he roared. ('Charge!')

'Attack!' cried Murx Espin.

The battle was on.

Swords clashed. Rocks flew. The sound of clashing weaponry and battle cries filled the night. The torches and flame-tipped arrows of the Guardians blazed through the dark sky and danced in the wind as the rain lashed down on all the combatants. From the watchtowers, the sentries proved to be great shots, successfully aiming arrow after arrow at their enemies despite the weather.

Gravelburn let out a piercing shout. *'Grat vu tur nash!'*

'Grat vu tur nash!' his warriors echoed, and more Rochgwars advanced forward, spreading themselves out to wreak as much havoc as possible.

The senior Guardians engaged the Rochgwars while the younger ones helped in any way they could, by shouting out warnings, or throwing rocks and other weapons at the Rochgwars. Despite their organised march, the Rochgwars had not been given a plan for when they were inside the base. Gravelburn had just told them to cause as much damage as possible. The Rochgwars fought but often found themselves isolated in losing two-on-one situations. So it was no surprise that they were slowly losing the fight.

When it looked to Gravelburn that he no longer had a chance to win, he ordered, *'Gung grata rothi!'*

The order was echoed and the Rochgwars executed a retreat. They linked up with Gargna and the Flygwars, who had been tasked with securing the outer perimeter. The fighting inside had been disorderly, but the retreat was not. Groups of Rochgwars engaged the Guardians while other groups pulled back, and they took it in turns to move to the rear. The rain continued to lash down as Gravelburn's men made it across the open ground to the edge of the forest in their second defeat.

Chapter Eight
All Going to Plan

It was nearly dawn and the Rochgwars were near their camp. They had trudged through the expansive forest and come out at the other side. From there they would make their way via the four tunnels that carved through the mountain they called Rochg Infini, before arriving at their base camp.

No one knew how tunnels came to exist. Some Rochgwarian historians said a great civilisation once existed here, with human slaves forced to dig the tunnels. Other legends described how the Great Rochgwarian god Rochg Warus had stuck his mighty hand into the mountain in anger, and the tunnels were said to be where his four fingers and thumb had breached the rock.

As the Rochgwars marched through one of the tunnels, they did so in fear. They had suffered losses and injuries, and had been repulsed yet again. There were certainly many things for Gravelburn to fume about.

They imagined that Gravelburn was inwardly cursing. They wondered if he was thinking in Old Rochgwarian again, and feared that when they got back, there might be a purge – where Gravelburn got rid of those that he thought had failed him in the battle.

But they could not have been further away from the truth.

Even though he had lost again, Gravelburn was humming an Old Rochgwarian folk song. While walking through the forest earlier, he had even listened out for the singing of birds.

He now seemed lost in his thoughts and was smiling from time to time.

Things were *definitely* going according to plan.

*   *   *

Three days later, the Rochgwars still did not fully understand the recent turn of events. One of these was the arrival of the Flygwars. How had Gravelburn found them? How did he intend to deploy them? And who was this Gargna they now had to take orders from? And just what exactly were these boulders that the Flygwars were now continually bringing into the camp? Where were they getting them from? The tunnels? Or were they bringing them down from the top of Rochg Infini?

Most worryingly, they did not understand why Gravelburn had now been seen smiling for days now, even though he had lost two battles in a row. Things were certainly amiss.

When they were not busy fighting, the Rochgwars would head for the tunnels and dig. They didn't know what exactly they were digging for, or why. Gravelburn had only told them to keep digging for rocks – the bigger the better. So the Rochgwars would return with large pieces and dump them at the corner of their camp, where a giant mound of rocks lay. Before battle, each of them would grab their own weapons, but also load their own packs with rocks that they could then use to hurl at the enemy.

The Rochgwars dug from the tunnels, and they went back and forth multiple times each day, transferring whatever they had dug out to the pile. It didn't escape them that while they were busy digging, Gravelburn had his eye on the Flygwars and the boulders they were bringing back.

'Grast vish tul nik?' one Rochgwar said to the one behind him, indicating at the Flygwars with a flick of his head, as they both walked to set down their rocks.

'Nie das tum,' was the reply, along with a shrug of the shoulders.

The Rochgwars were always told to get on with their tasks, but these two now observed the Flygwars out of the corners

41

of their eyes, while they cradled their rocks. Their footsteps slowed to a stroll. Gravelburn and the Flygwars all seemed to be standing around a boulder, and the leader looked very excited. To the Rochgwars, they all just seemed to be standing around watching a big piece of rock.

The two Rochgwars watched intently as others overtook them. The boulder seemed to be vibrating slowly. The first blinked in disbelief. No, his eyes were not playing tricks on him. The pair could now see the boulder moving back and forth. It seemed to expand as it rolled, and then suddenly shaped itself into a Rochgwar who got up, looked around hesitantly, then ran off.

'*Uth der mighk!*' the first Rochgwar roared and dropped his collection of rocks.

'*Oof!*' said the second as the rocks landed on his feet. He then dropped his own pile of rocks. '*Oof! Oof repa tus! Dah neet!*' He hobbled around in pain.

42

A commotion like this would have normally drawn attention, and a stern word, but Gravelburn was too busy celebrating. The sides of his mouth were turned upward, higher than any Rochgwar could ever remember they had been.

Chapter Nine
The Mysterious Figure

Robin was in the bunk, putting away his things. That didn't take long, as he had few prized possessions beyond what he immediately needed. Armour. Spear. Dagger. Club. Boots. *All done*. There was a break in the training until it was time for lunch, and while his friends had chosen to continue playing outside, Robin was just a little tired for that today and wanted to have a bit of peace and quiet.

It would be a nice short break away from the usual things. Heath's constant chatter. Ember's constant advice about 'being prepared' – Ember was nice, but sometimes he went on a bit too much. Nitro's 'I-Spy' games. Cut and Fil egging each other on, trying to see who was the tougher one. Robin liked his friends, but sometimes he also liked being away from them a little bit.

He sat on the floor and carefully removed his boots, taking care not to fray the laces. *They used to belong to your father*, Murx Espin had told him as he handed them over. Before putting them away, Robin closed his eyes and held them between his fingers, as if to feel a connection with the man he had never known.

He stretched out on the floor. It was a Guardian rule that one was not to be found sleeping on the bed during the day, so Robin made a bit of space for himself to lie down from among the things that littered the floor. The room was always neat during the daily first inspection, but in their haste to get ready for training the junior Guardians always ended up leaving it messy. Hence the need for the second inspection before sunset.

Robin could feel fatigue from the morning's training take hold of him. The morning's training had been on combat skills. *Block. Punch. Step across. Throw.* They had done so many of these repetitions that the words continued to echo in the

45

back of his mind, even as Robin stared at the ceiling and let his thoughts run freely. Some of the senior Guardians had been in this base all their lives. Others were from bases elsewhere, but had transferred over when they graduated up the ranks. Would he be here his whole lifetime? Or was there a life beyond the walls of the base? *Block. Punch. Step across. Throw ...*

Robin could feel his muscles tighten as his body rested; he was drifting, drifting away. *Block. Punch. Step across. Throw.* He was losing in the battle to stay awake. *Block. Punch. Step acro...*

Out of the corner of his eyes, he saw a figure flash past in the hallway outside. Robin shot up.

He caught a glimpse of a foot as it disappeared around the hallway. Robin gave chase, but as he rounded the first corner, and the next, he saw nothing. Had he dreamt it? He had definitely heard footsteps. And he had definitely seen a foot.

He needed to tell somebody.

Most of the group leaders were having a meeting in the Great Hall. Robin was about to enter, but before he could knock, he decided that it might not be a good time. Instead he observed from the outside, standing awkwardly at the door, listening for a good moment to interrupt.

Murx Espin, representatives from the other bases and key leaders were having a discussion.

'We have to expect another attack,' Robin overheard.

There were murmurings and raised voices, but he could not link the words with who spoke them.

'The OP is in position.'

'They're too strong. The ratio is not in our favour.'

'What is the DPR for the E-group?'

Robin imagined leaders sitting down, arguing over imaginary situations. To him, it was a lot of words.

'This is ridiculous,' thought Robin. 'They are all wasting time talking when they could actually be doing something. They are all losing precious time here, running through options when they need to decide soon.'

Something came to his mind. It was a thought so strong, it made Robin temporarily forget his manners and he burst into the meeting room.

The seated leaders swivelled around.

'What are you doing here?' Murx Espin said. Usually he spoke kindly, but the sharp tone in his voice then told Robin that he was not happy with the interruption at the moment.

Robin smiled. 'I have an idea that will blow your minds.'

Chapter Ten
The Dawning

Robin knew he had only thirty seconds or less before he was ordered out. He quickly composed himself.

'I have been listening to you discuss plans to defend the base from Rochgwar attacks,' said Robin. 'Here's what we know and should do …'

'Rochgwars inbound!' a Guardian burst in the Hall shouting.

The hall emptied as all the Guardians rushed out. They grabbed their weapons – claymores, bows, maces, axes, lances – and readied themselves for the next wave of attacks.

Robin stood addressing a circle of empty chairs.

'Oh come on!' Robin whinged. 'I was right in the middle of my plan! This ALWAYS happens to me, like the time when I had a really good dream and then someone woke me up before the end! Or the time Heath revealed the punchline to my exciting joke. And …'

While Robin seethed with rage and blabbered on, something else was going on outside.

*   *   *

Murx Espin had called for foot patrols around the base during the day after the second Rochgwar attack days ago. One of the sentries from the eastern watchtower had spotted movement and alerted the foot patrols to investigate. This time the Guardians had advance warning.

Robin had finally snapped out of his craziness. 'What am I doing here, talking to empty seats, pretending the leaders

51

are listening to me?' He dashed to his room to get his weapons.

Robin could hear the roar of the charging Rochgwars. What plan did they have this time? Were the gates to the base protected?

Robin laced his boots up, and took his axe and shield. The Guardians were all assigned an area to defend, and Robin was now late to his post. As he made his way to his battle station, he stopped outside the bunk that another group of juniors slept in.

He could hear something.

It was some sort of a knocking sound, like knuckles against a wall. Robin traced for the direction of the sound, and he saw that there was something under John's bed.

He advanced slowly and peered underneath.

Robin decided he must be going mad. Could a rock make this noise? Perhaps there was a fox or other animal behind it, struggling to get out from underneath the bed. But Robin could not see any.

It must have only taken three seconds, but one side of the bed was suddenly lifted off the ground and there was now a fully-grown Rochgwar standing in front of Robin. Robin reared back in shock and then quickly swung with his axe, smashing it into pieces before the Rochgwar could react.

He then stepped backwards, examining the pieces on the floor, and not believing what had just taken place. But as he headed to the battle area, his heart raced with nervous excitement.

He knew. He knew!

Chapter Eleven
The Third Attack

The Rochgwars were using artillery attacks from outside the base. They rolled out their catapults, and launched their rocks at or over the perimeter walls. It must have taken them ages to move these machines through the forest. The rocks were soaked in some sort of sticky liquid and set alight before they were launched, so it was raining rock fire inside the base.

'We'll need to take out their catapults! To the perimeter walls!' group commanders ordered their men into position.

They ran up the steps to the watchtowers, where separate paths led them along the perimeter walls. The Rochgwars soon faced Guardians along the whole length of the walls, shooting down at them with flame-tipped arrows. There was not enough space for every Guardian, and those that did not manage to get up formed a long human chain, passing up arrows and other weapons – anything that could be hurled at the Rochgwars. Injured Guardians were also helped down and replacements stepped up to take their place.

The Guardians of C-group were sent as reserves to the gates in case Rochgwars broke through. They were huddled together closer to the walls, which meant they were less likely to get hit by the rocks. But the Rochgwars weren't the only ones with catapults. The Guardians of E-group wheeled out their own catapults, modified to hurl javelins high over the walls. The Rochgwars faced a harassing storm of arrows and javelins from beyond the walls, and were – for the moment – being contained. But they were still scoring some hits.

'Argh!' screamed a Guardian as a rock whacked the side of his head. 'Medic!' screamed the one next to him as he fell.

'Garth! John! Reinforce the line!' ordered a team commander. Two Guardians dashed up to take the two empty places along the wall. The injured pair were helped down and given help.

From the perimeter walls, the view of the scene below was one of chaos. Rochgwars tried to bring down the gates with a battering ram, but the gates held firm, and they were constantly met by arrows and javelins. Gravelburn's battle plan had called for Rochgwars to attack the base while the Flygwars cut off any outside help, but none of that was going to plan. The Rochgwars could not get in Delton, and they were all clustered together outside with the Flygwars, making them easy targets for the Guardians.

'Gargna! Um rath shem hrwat!' Gravelburn roared. He hated losing.

A small team of Flygwars made their way to one wall and started scaling it. They hovered and reached for points in the wall, making their way upwards more quickly than Rochgwars would have.

'Kreeth ne sar um grath tee!' Gravelburn roared again.

The Rochgwar catapults now concentrated all their fire on the same side. The Guardians there found themselves hit with the full firepower of their enemies, which meant they had to take cover every now and then. The number of arrows coming down from that side was reduced.

The Flygwars were halfway up the walls. For many Guardians, this was the first time they had seen Flygwars in action. They watched them advance, wings beating furiously as they leapt from point to point. Each time the Guardians looked over, the Flygwars had advanced. The leading Flygwars were so close that the Guardians could see their menacing faces, but they were having difficulties scaling the last section of the wall. They had to be careful not just to avoid the Guardian arrows, but also to avoid being hit by the stones that were being launched by the Rochgwar catapults.

If there is a breach in the defensive line, there might be a chance for them, John thought.

Robin had arrived at the scene of the battle while dodging pieces of flaming rock randomly raining down from the sky. A team commander yelled for him to take cover, and quickly called for him to come over to the sides, where it was safer. Robin soon found himself next to Heath and Fil, who were passing arrows up the line.

'Have you seen John?' Robin shouted to them.

'Who?'

'John! From the teen Guardians!'

Fil pointed John out.

Chapter Twelve
Traitor!

Robin dashed up the steps to the watchtower and along the path. He had to dodge past Guardians taking cover from rocks and reloading their bows, and as he scuttled towards John, he noticed the teen Guardian had his bow in one hand, but was not loading any arrows with the other. He was just crouching down and springing up, making the motion of shooting. But not actually firing anything. In the heat of the battle, his deception was not noticed.

Next to John, Garth now had a direct shot at one of the Flygwars. He wedged himself firmly against the wall, pulled back on his bow, tensioned his body to avoid jerking upwards on the shot and then carefully lined the tip of the arrow with the Flygwar's chest.

'What!' he shouted as the arrow swerved on release.

John had sidled over and was now trying to throw him over the wall! Garth clung precariously, his body almost horizontal, as John grabbed his boots and kept trying to lift them even higher.

'Are you crazy?' he shouted.

It was a wrestling match. One held on with all his might. The other lifted and pushed with all his might. The momentum swung from one to the other, back and forth. In the end, a pair of boots and their owner were sent flying over the wall and tumbled down the sides, taking down some Flygwars in the process.

The remaining few Flygwars were now left exposed lower down, where they were easily picked off with arrows. One screamed in pain when an arrow pierced its wings, and when it fell it crumbled on impact into a pile of rocks. When Robin briefly looked over, he saw that there was a mound of rocks at the base of the wall. And two human hands poked out from beneath them.

Robin took cover temporarily, his heart racing. 'Thanks,' said Garth. 'But why did you throw him over?'

*   *   *

John had knocked into some Flygwars on his way down, and also landed on some Rochgwars, so it was not a soft landing.

'Aargh! That really hurt!' John shouted.

Dear reader, do you remember the first sentence in this story? Well, that's what John landed on. Or imagine John was saved by a family of porcupines. Or maybe that he landed on a cactus bed. Ah well, that's what happened.

The battle was certainly not going in Gravelburn's favour. His troops were massed outside the base in this third battle, with no way of getting in, while they were being attacked and picked off.

'Ragradh!' he cursed, and the Rochgwars executed a hasty retreat. The catapults were wheeled away, still firing as the frontline Rochgwars made vain attempts to harass the Guardians. Then the catapults launched cursory rocks as the Rochgwars in front of them pulled back. They alternated this until they were out of range of the Guardian arrows and javelins. The Guardians jeered their retreat.

'Good job, Guardians!' cried Murx Espin. 'We have shown fortitude, and defended against huge numbers. We will never let them prevail!'

'Hurraaaaah!' The cheering roars could be heard by the Rochgwars outside Delton as they pulled back.

'Now let every man and woman and child tend to those who need help. Any weapons on the ground should be collected and brought to the armoury. Be on your guard though. I want sentries to continue keeping watch. They may only be making a feint. They might be pretending to retreat, before attacking again. Don't let up! Get archers on the walls on standby.

'Command group, head for the Hall. We have to discuss these developments.'

Robin was about to help pick up fallen arrows and javelins, as well as the possessions of the wounded, when Murx Espin called for him.

'Robin! Leave the weapons. You're coming with us to the Hall.'

Chapter Thirteen
Reunion

It was hard to march in step with a twisted ankle. And every breath that he took seemed to cause a sharp stabbing pain in his sides. If all that wasn't bad enough, he was continually being shoved from behind when his movement slowed. So it was actually relief for John to be pushed to the ground when they finally arrived at their destination.

'Grystvaruch!' a Rochgwar snarled.

John inhaled sharply and grimaced. He slowly pushed himself onto his knees and found himself staring at Gravelburn.

'Where was the Rochgwar we left you? You were supposed to help him open the Delton gates at the sun's peak, so that we could get in to attack.'

'I don't know! When I got back to my room there were just bits of rock on the floor. It must not have regrown properly.'

'Nonsense!' fumed Gravelburn. 'It works fine! You said you would work for us. But you led us into a trap! You left us trapped and ambushed outside the gates! You're going to pay for this!'

'I didn't betray you! I went around looking for a way, an excuse, to open the gates to Delton. I even tried to get into the watchtower to warn you. But you must have been spotted on the way here!'

'Guards! Take him to the tunnels!' Gravelburn snarled. 'Let the traitor spend the next three days digging rock with his hands till they go red and sore. That will teach him to betray us!'

John suddenly felt himself dragged backwards by the backplate of his armour. Two Rochgwars pulled him along the dusty, rocky ground. *Oh well, at least I don't have to walk,* he thought.

He had never been this far out of Delton, let alone to the Rochgwar base. So as he was dragged along, he took notice of the new sights and sounds. He noticed a huge mound of rocks in one corner. A long line of Rochgwars walked to and from this pile, dumping the rocks they carried in their arms. Elsewhere, Rochgwars with wings flew in bigger rocks. They all stopped what they were doing, and turned and stared at the unusual sight of the human in their midst.

'All right?' John weakly lifted a hand and waved sarcastically as he found himself the centre of attention.

After about fifty paces or so, they came to a tunnel. It was dimly lit, with a burning torch at one side. He was dragged further and further in and finally thrown like a rock onto the ground.

66

'Me wish Gravelburn said to put him in the training tunnel,' said one Rochgwar.

'Me too. Fun to watch. But no. Let's go,' replied the other.

'Keep digging!' a voice echoed down the tunnel.

John had no idea where it had come from. But someone must be observing those in the tunnel. He'd had enough contact with Rochgwars for one day and did not want to be thumped any more. He scratched feebly at the sides of the tunnel, mimicking the actions of the Rochgwar next to him.

The Rochgwar turned and watched. Then he edged closer until John could feel his sneering breath across his own face. He dared not to turn at first, but he sensed the Rochgwar was waiting for him to react. 'Don't look!' the voice in his head said. 'Just keep digging!' But the Rochgwar didn't move, and John decided that he couldn't go on like this, digging with a head hovering around his shoulders. He stopped and slowly returned the gaze.

'So it is you,' Grunted finally said, fixing him with a stare.

Chapter Fourteen
Truths in the Tunnel

John froze. 'What are you doing here?'

'I could ask the same question of you,' replied Grunted. 'Except your presence here already tells me the answer. You obviously didn't execute Gravelburn's plan properly.'

Grunted turned around and walked back to his spot, musing to himself. 'Two attacks to create a diversion to smuggle a Rochgwar to you, and from what I heard, you couldn't even get it to do a simple thing like open gates.'

John could not stand there and just take the insults without giving one back.

'So they brought useless me here ... I guess that makes me as useless as you.'

Grunted flinched and was about to respond when the guard's voice echoed down the tunnel. 'You two down there! Keep digging! No talking!'

Grunted shoved John aside as he headed towards the Rochgwar guard. When they were nose to nose, Grunted intoned, 'Listen here. I used to be the deputy commander of this army. You probably don't recognise me because you couldn't recognise my face from standing twenty rows back. Now take a look at my face and remember it. Gravelburn may have banished me here, but nobody – nobody – tells me to pick rocks. If you want an ex-deputy commander to pick rocks, *make me*.' He let his stare hang for what seemed like forever, then walked back to his spot and sat down.

The guard did nothing. Then Grunted slowly retraced the path back to his position and sat down. John recognised it as a good moment to pretend to befriend Grunted. It would save him from digging. So much to Grunted's surprise, he sat down next to him and started to ask questions.

'What's everyone digging for, anyway?'

Grunted took the bait. He started talking. John knew the guard did not dare to challenge Grunted, so as long as he kept Grunted talking, he himself would not have to dig either.

'Legend tells us that the early Rochgwars were formed from huge rocks thrown out by Rochg Infini, the Great Fire Mountain. Rochgwars believe that after these rocks broke off into smaller pieces, these pieces regenerated and formed into more Rochgwars. The bigger pieces become Flygwars. Gravelburn wants the Rochgwars to keep digging, so he can have a bigger army of Flygwars and Rochgwars.'

'Do you believe it is true?'

Grunted took a deep breath and exhaled. 'Look at us Rochgwars. We are formed partly from cold stone. We keep attacking you and we keep getting beaten down. How is it there never seems to be fewer and fewer Rochgwars?'

John had no answer.

'Because it is true.'

John could not speak. He could not fully understand what Grunted was telling him.

'You mean when Guardians fight Rochgwars and break them into little pieces, each little piece later grows back into another Rochgwar? If that is true, wouldn't there just be more and more Rochgwars growing out from each defeated one?'

Grunted explained, 'Each piece has to be a minimum size in order to regenerate. After it is smaller past a certain size, it cannot become a Rochgwar. It's just not possible. You cannot make a Rochgwar from a pebble.'

'So let me get this straight …' John just had difficulty understanding what he was hearing. 'Each Rochgwar crumbles when it is defeated. Each piece, if it is big enough, grows back after a while to become another Rochgwar.'

'You're getting it. You're not as stupid as you look.'

'How long does it take for a piece of rock to become a Rochgwar?'

'I don't know. Maybe within the passing of a moon to another. Maybe not. Sometimes it's fast and sometimes it's slow. Nobody knows why. All I know is, I've never run out of Rochgwars in my army. Maybe those rocks with wings will know more about this. Maybe we'll get lucky when we're digging and find a few more.'

Chapter Fifteen
A Shining Light

Meanwhile, Robin was holding court, telling all the other Guardians what he had seen. He was felt very nervous – all the older and experienced Guardians were listening to him!

'It grew?' That was one of the questions he was asked when he finished.

Robin nodded. 'How long did it take to grow?'

'It shook for about a few moments and then it just suddenly just ... popped ... became a Rochgwar. But the kind of Rochgwar with wings.'

'And you smashed it into pieces?' Robin nodded. There was murmuring among the listeners.

Murx Espin faced the other leaders. 'This is grave news indeed. It may explain why the Rochgwars are digging in the tunnels. They want reinforcements.'

'We have to go destroy the tunnels,' Lex Cerberus insisted.

'We have to consider ... do we have the capability to march to their base and attack it?' Hinx Matr asked.

'Are the Guardians capable of fighting the Rochgwars on their own territory?' Sarg Ribaurus, the logistics officer asked.

Murx Espin looked on solemnly. 'Does anyone here still remember the mission nearly eight years ago? We tried to move explosive material through the tunnels to destroy the Rochgwar base. I'm not sure we want to lose fifty-six men again. I still remember every single one of them. Reb Talanus. Lib Rawf. Shim Yibar. Bul Posiron …'

A messenger burst in the Great Hall. 'The OP reports that Rochgwars were seen moving out of their base!'

Murx Espin snapped out of his reminiscence. 'Prepare the defences! Make sure there are archers at the walls!' he commanded.

'This is going to be like the last time. I'm going to enjoy trapping them outside the base again and picking them off one by one!' Enos Pastulus, an excited Guardian team leader, rubbed his hands with glee.

'No!' Robin suddenly shouted. The word just came out of his mouth like that, before he could stop it. 'We can't just stay inside the base. We have to meet them outside and fight. And then we have to keep moving out all the way to the tunnels to eventually destroy them.'

'We can't fight all the way to their base!' Sarg Ribaurus protested. 'Why don't we just stay within our base, well-protected, and fight them? What does this eight-year-old know about battle tactics?'

Robin ignored him. 'Don't you see? The Rochgwars keep sending wave after wave of attacks. They don't care if they lose or win. They have enough Rochgwars to keep coming. But we can't just hide in the base waiting for them to come. It doesn't matter if we keep winning these little battles or outnumber them. We'll run out of weapons. We'll run out of food. We'll be trapped inside here and have to give up. That is their plan! To starve us into giving up!'

There was a long silence as everyone considered Robin's words.

Murx Espin was the first to speak. 'So what do you suggest?'

*   *   *

'Jolly good, old boy!'

'I can't believe he's only eight years old!'

'What a classic!'

These comments were made by three elderly Guardian lieutenants after Robin spoke. No one was exactly sure what some of them actually meant, but Robin was feeling very pleased after telling his idea to the leaders. There was not much time to ask questions because the Rochgwars were making good progress and were about three hours away. The meeting quickly disbanded.

'Robin!' Murx Espin walked over and put a hand on Robin's shoulder. 'Good plan. You sure you can handle it?'

'Yes. I'm nearly nine now. Actually, in a few days from now it will be my birthday. So, yes, I think I can.'

Birthdays in the base were small affairs, usually spent playing Nitro's boring 'I-Spy' games, being pranked by Heath, or watching everyone get into a massive stick fight started by either Cut or Fil that ended up with someone being hurt. Robin was feeling optimistic that his birthday might be remembered in history as the time when the Guardians finally defeated the Rochgwars once and for all.

'Good luck. *Yhet juvicht abels*.'

Chapter Sixteen
The Fourth Attack

Robin had no idea what Murx Espin was saying as they parted. The last few words seemed lost in his thick bushy beard. The base was a hive of activity. The Guardians were preparing madly getting every weapon they could get their hands on. There was so much clattering that team leaders had to shout above the noise to be heard, which only meant they made more noise that others had to shout over.

The Rochgwars were marching with their usual chants and singing. There was no need to be stealthy now. They knew the Guardians would be expecting them. They were marching in bright daylight and could be seen from afar. So they rejoiced and sang their Old Roghwar war songs.

Vee vull vee vull Rochg yew!
Vee vull vee vull Rochg yew!

Gravelburn rallied his troops in a loud rendition of the popular war song, 'Ten Rochgwars'. The lyrics were in Old Rochgwarian, of course, but an English translation might be something like this:

Ten Rochgwars, taking down the wall
Ten Rochgwars, taking down the wall
And if one of them should accidentally fall,
There'll still be some more Rochgwars taking down the wall!

The Rochgwars were in such an excited state before they even got to 'Wind the Catapult Up'.

Wind the catapult up
Wind the catapult up
Launch! Launch!
Plak! Plak! Plak!

But as they neared the Guardian base, the singing suddenly stopped. The Rochgwars had expected that they would

81

assault the base as they normally did, and find the Guardians holding them off from within. Instead they found Guardians waiting for them in the open ground, on what used to be their old FEBA. Their rear lines had not even cleared the forest yet. Surely the Guardians would not engage them in the open, where the Rochgwars had a fighting advantage?

They would.

'Grag grillaskah!' Gravelburn roared.

The Rochgwars charged forward. But the lack of space meant they had to advance a line at a time, and could not broaden out to take advantage of their numbers, or flank their enemies, so the Guardians easily picked them off. Each line of Rochgwars was met by a wall of maces and similar weaponry, and each replacement Rochgwar suffered the same fate. The Rochgwars crumbled as they advanced.

'Grush gill gata!' Gravelburn's battle cry echoed throughout. He was definitely not sounding happy.

Robin's plan was working well. The catapults that the Rochgwars wheeled along to battle could not be used in the forest because of the tree cover, and were rendered useless. And the Rochgwars did not have the fighting space to deploy more than a line of warriors at a time. But even though they were winning, the Guardians now retreated back to their base.

Gravelburn sensed the advantage swing to him. The Guardians were giving up ground. The Rochgwars advanced forward into the open ground where they would be better at fighting. They moved their catapults forward into the open where they could now be used. It was time for phase two of Robin's plan.

'Robin!' Murx Espin shouted for him. The boy, soon to be nine, ran over to him.

'Are you ready?' Robin nodded.

'Get your team ready and move out.'

'Are you all going to be okay?' Robin asked, slightly fearfully. He wondered if there was going to be a base of Guardians when he returned.

Murx Espin gave him a big hug. 'We'll be fine. There are fewer of them around now. We can hold them off. Now go – we need you. Good luck and be safe.'

The Guardians and Rochgwars were engaging again, this time on open ground. Amidst all the fighting, shouting and bashing, a group of eight junior Guardians flanked the battle area, slipping past it undetected, behind the Rochgwar catapults and into the forest. Towards the Rochgwar base.

Chapter Seventeen
Linked for Life

'Have you decided?' Grunted asked the two Rochgwars. A small group of them had been left behind. Gravelburn was no longer angry with Grunted, and had put him in charge before leaving for battle. Grunted, in turn, had assigned two of the Rochgwars to handle matters.

'Well sir, we have a small scout section positioned there,' one said, pointing to where he had meant on the sketch he made in the earth. 'The others are all divided them among the four tunnels.'

Grunted fumed. 'Why have you divided all the Rochgwars into the four tunnels? Two of the tunnels have already been abandoned. What will they be digging for? You dummy! Just put one or two Rochgwars to stand guard in the abandoned tunnels in case the Guardians come that way. Then get the rest to continue digging in the useful one. Do I have to spell it all out for you?' And with that, he gave the Rochgwar a massive blow that broke him into pieces. The pieces crumbled to the ground.

'Hey! That's not fair!' said the piece that used to be the head, before the face dimmed to become a smooth surface. The other Rochgwar hastily gathered the main pieces and hurried them to the rock pile in the corner of the base.

John looked on, stunned. Then he gathered himself and asked, 'Why didn't we all go and attack Delton? I could have taken you there and helped you attack them. Why did Gravelburn leave us behind? And how do you know the Guardians will be coming here?'

Grunted sneered. 'You fool. Gravelburn knows they will come. He has already prepared for that. It's all part of the Great Plan. Gravelburn is always one step ahead. We may be made of rock, but we don't have rocks for brains. The

Guardians know that they can't just stay in their base. Sooner or later, they have to come out here and meet us on our own turf.'

John persisted with his questions. 'But suppose they decide to fight your Rochgwars from inside the base?'

Grunted sighed. He had a face similar to someone who'd just had to babysit twenty baby Rochgwars and listen to childish questions.

'Look. The Guardians are coming. Even if they are not coming to fight, they are coming for you, fleshling. They may be coming to rescue you. I don't know if 'rescue' is even the right word. If not, they'll be coming for you anyway, to get you back, to question you and find out why you betrayed them. Do you not think that Gravelburn has thought of this already? There may be things you don't yet know, or don't yet understand. You may not know the whole picture. But I'll tell you this. Gravelburn is always ... one step ahead! By the

87

time the Guardians find out, they'll already be walking into his trap. It's too late. *Arghahaha*!'

John froze. Things were certainly moving faster than he could understand. But he realised that now he had betrayed the Guardians, there was no turning back for him. He had told Gravelburn about details such as the guard routine, and he had tried to throw one of the Guardians over the wall. John's fate had been decided. He was stuck with the Rochgwars forever.

Chapter Eighteen
Spotted

They had been walking for what seemed like forever and would soon be nearing the Rochgwar camp. The eight junior Guardians, led by Robin, could only hope that the enemy base would be deserted, and that all of the Rochgwars would be at the main battle. The eight of them had made good ground, but were tired after having done some fighting earlier before their long march. Their faces were tired, and their bodies hunched from the effort. But they had to keep going. They were surely near their objective. They had nearly run out of water, and now their stomachs were rumbling. As they approached the far edge of the forest, Robin thought he saw something: a misty figure.

He blinked. Were his eyes playing tricks on him? Was it a supernatural figure? 'Ghost!' Robin whispered. But none of the other Guardians seemed to be aware of its presence.

Either it was because they had their heads down, or Robin was just imagining it. The ghost hovered closer and seemed like it was trying to say something to him. Robin didn't want to hear it. He wanted to ignore it altogether. But these were the scraps he heard:

'Robin ... I ... mother ... Gravelburn ... father ...'

Robin felt scared when he heard these words. 'Was that ghost my mother? And was it saying Gravelburn is my father?' None of the other Guardians seemed to have seen it. Robin looked to see if the ghost was there but all he saw was ...

'Rochgwars incoming!'

Robin snapped out of his dream world immediately. As the Guardians prepared their maces, Robin charged with his. He knocked a Rochgwar with a single swing of his mace. But suddenly he found himself knocked to the ground, and

90

another Rochgwar was on top of him. Just as the stone monster was about to strike, there was a smash and Robin saw the monster's head explode into fragments of stone. Ember had attacked the Rochgwar just before it was about to land a blow. It had not seen that coming.

The Rochgwar's comrade responded angrily to this, and so he picked up some rocks and threw them. They smacked into Cut, temporarily stunning him. But the Guardians managed to team up on it and soon it crumbled.

The last two monsters were falling back now. Slick picked up his bow and pulled back with an arrow.

Whizz! The arrow flew through the air and hit the fleeing Rochgwar in its soft midsection, one of the traditional weak spots of a Rochwar. *'Argh!'* It screamed as it was hit and crumbled.

91

The danger was over for now. The Guardians soon found themselves in a small clearing which led off to four different tunnels.

'Let's have a rest here,' said Robin. Half of them should have kept watch, while the other half rested, before swapping around, but they all so tired that they all fell asleep.

Soon there were eight dozing Guardians. They were watched by something in one of the tunnels. It quietly slinked away and headed towards the Rochgwar base.

'They are having a rest,' the Rochgwar scout eventually reported to Grunted.

'Just as Gravelburn predicted, they have come,' smiled Grunted. 'Send in the second wave of Rochgwars!'

Chapter Nineteen
Before the Tunnels

Slick suddenly sat up. How had they all fallen asleep? How long had they been asleep for? He hastily woke everyone up. They could hear faint shouting in the distance.

'What is that?' he said to nobody in particular. 'Everybody! Get up!'

'I don't know, but I don't think it's good, whatever it is,' said Robin.

'The rumbling's getting louder, we need to go now,' shouted Slick.

'Go now – but where?' asked Robin.

'There's nowhere to go!' hissed Cut.

'Are you dumb?' said Heath. 'There are four tunnels ahead of us, Cut!'

'Yes, I know,' said Cut, 'I'm not dumb. And I can see for myself. But that's where the rumbling is coming from! No one will want to go in them!'

'You two stop bickering!' said Slick. 'I agree with Heath. We should go into the tunnels in pairs. There are eight of us, so we should be able to do that. We can't just sit here waiting for things to happen.'

'Slick and Heath are right,' agreed Robin. 'We have to move on to get further. We can't just sit here and avoid going into these tunnels.'

'Then what are we waiting for?' said Slick, pleased to take the credit. 'What do the rest of you think?'

'It's dangerous.'

'It's witty.'

'It's smart.'

'I told you,' grumbled Cut to Slick. 'They don't want to do it. Cowards!'

'Quit complaining,' said Slick.

Just when they were deciding what to do, three Rochgwars poked their heads out of a tunnel. Their nervous, puzzled looks turned to looks of dislike. One Rochgwar launched a rock at the Guardians. 'Ow!' said Cut as he was stunned.

'Well, at least we won't have to listen to the grumbling any more,' chuckled Slick to Robin.

'Look out!' shouted Robin to Slick. But it was too late. Another large rock flew through the air and landed on his head. *Wham!* 'That's two Guardians down now,' sighed Robin. 'Concentrate, everyone!'

'Roger!' exclaimed Fil as he was hit by a rock and became the third casualty.

'Urghhh!' grunted Robin as he charged forward, making easy work of two Rochgwars with one swipe of his mace. The last one now retreated, only to be trampled on by twenty-seven oncoming Rochgwars. Slick and Cut had now recovered, and the Guardians were smashing Rochgwars to dust, or launching arrows at them.

'You're outnumbered!' shouted the Rochgwar commander, just as five of his soldiers fell around him, followed by a further five.

'Forward!' shouted Robin. The Guardians ran towards the last few Rochgwars, taking them out as they ran. 'I think that's the last of them,' said Robin as he swung his weapon.

'I wouldn't be sure about that!' said Fil, who had recovered.

'Look! It's those flying Rochgwars!' said Slick, pointing at the approaching monsters.

'Hey, you! Stop right there!' hissed the Flygwars.

'No chance!' shouted Heath, smashing one with his sword when it got close. Together with Slick and Nitro, they launched into a whole combination of thrusts, jumps and jabs which took out most of the Flygwars. It was an amazing dance partnership with props, and would have earned scores of perfect tens had any of the senior Guardians been watching. Soon only one last Flygwar remained, and as it retreated, it found itself right in the path of Cut. *Crunch!* Tiny pieces littered the floor.

'They just keep coming!' cried Jack.

'We know!' said just about everyone else there, including more Rochgwars that had just emerged out from the tunnels.

'Goodbye!' roared Slick as he smacked a Rochgwar. It flew into the air and landed on another. Both ended up as a pile of rocks.

'Ouch!' said Cut as he was being hit by the madly-beating wings of a Flygwar. He was slapped from wing to wing and had to retreat. Some of the others helped him fight it off.

'Take that!' shouted Fil as he whacked a Rochgwar straight into the air. The stone warrior fell back, tripped over some rocks, fell down and then crumbled away.

'Keep – pushing – forward!' shouted Robin above the noise.

'Roger!' said Heath even more loudly.

'Who's Roger?' dumbly asked the Rochgwar he was fighting.

98

'No one's Roger!' shouted Slick.

'Oh, not again!' said the Rochgwar as he saw an arrow fly towards him.

It looked like the Rochgwars were winning. 'We're outnumbered!' said Jack. There were definitely more stone monsters than junior Guardians. If the Rochgwars won this fight, this part of the mission would fail and Delton might eventually fall. The Guardians had to do something to prevent that. A Rochgwar screeched (well, only his head actually) as it was sent flying backwards by Robin.

The Guardians had to display courage and determination to fight their way out of this. And they did. More and more of the stone warriors turned into fragments and dust as the junior Guardians smashed through their ranks. The Rochgwars were nervous because their numbers were decreasing.

Soon it was clear that the tide was turning in favour of the Guardians. Ten minutes later, it looked like the Guardians were standing on a new cobblestone road!

'Ow!' complained Slick as he tripped over a stone monster's head. 'You think that hurt? I just tasted boot!' said the head. 'Have a second helping!' said Cut as he kicked it away.

'OWWWwwww ... !' screamed the head as it flew into the distance.

Chapter Twenty
Entering the Tunnels

The fighting was over for now, but the Guardians still had choices to make about how to press on with their mission.

'How will we decide which tunnel to go through? Should we go as a group, or split up?' thought Robin as he sat down, his mind aching. He looked up to see his team squabbling like crazy. Everyone was fatigued by now and not making the right choices.

'I want to go in this one!'

'No, me!'

'Be quiet everyone!' shouted Robin. They all turned to look at him. 'How about I blindfold all of you, then you hold hands with a random person and head off into a tunnel? That seems the fairest way.'

'Sounds reasonable!'

'Okay!'

'No, let's not do that! I don't hold hands!'

Robin sighed and rolled his eyes. The air bristled with comments – some good and some bad. Everyone had an opinion. Some didn't have an opinion and just decided to disagree with everything to sound like they had one. Others didn't really have a useful opinion – they were just speaking their thoughts aloud. Eventually Robin decided that he could, and should – as leader of this group – make the decisions and tell them what to do. Never mind if it made him the bad guy.

'Sorted?' asked Robin. 'Sorted,' grumbled some of the rest of the team. Into the tunnels they went, in pairs.

*   *   *

All they could see was dark. They had been walking for a long time. The two Guardians made their way across the tunnel with their arms outstretched, feeling their way around. One of them stumbled over something bumpy and fell over. Suddenly the other fell down too and both lay sprawled on the floor.

'What was that?' asked one.

'I don't know,' said the other.

There was a pause before either spoke.

'Do you think we should take off our blindfolds yet?'

There was another long pause.

'I guess,' said Slick.

'Look!' pointed out Jack. 'I see light!'

They froze. That could only mean there might be Rochgwars ahead. They carefully made their way towards the exit. Who knew what awaited them? The two Guardians didn't see any activity as they edged closer, but it didn't stop them from being cautious. They advanced slowly, weapons at the ready. Slick motioned for Jack to get behind him.

Slick tried to look outside the cave; he couldn't get a good view, but he saw piles of rocks. It wasn't a comforting sign but he decided they had to investigate. He signalled for Jack still to remain close behind. They moved forward, one step at a time. At every point Slick was sure that this looked just like a typical Rochgwar ambush, and he half-expected that when he emerged out into the open, he would find himself in the kill zone, with all sorts of Rochgwars appearing from hidden positions aiming their weapons at him. He need to advance cautiously, but all the time making sure he had an escape route.

The Rochgwars were doing a good job of remaining hidden. It was a waiting game. Slick waited near the exit and tried to listen out for movement but the Rochgwars were not giving anything away. Occasionally he heard the piercing cry of an eagle – had it spotted something hiding among the trees?

Things were going nowhere and Slick decided that at least one of them had to exit the cave. They could at least get a better view and report back to the others, or link up with them if they arrived.

He indicated to Jack that the latter should stay in the cave. Slick cautiously moved out first, weapon at the ready, and eyes continually scanning. There were broken rocks everywhere. The place looked strangely familiar.

'Have we been here before?' asked Jack, who emerged beside him.

'Yes!' said Slick, dropping his weapon. 'We started here!'

They groaned.

*   *   *

It was brighter in the second tunnel. But it was no use to the two Guardians there, who had also forgotten to remove their blindfolds. Slowly and steadily they inched forward. 'I can feel something!' said one.

'Me too!' said the other.

'It's a bit sharp!' said the first.

'I agree!' said the second.

'There's a funny smell in here! Smells like one of my stink bombs!'

The second Guardian sniffed the air. It was true – there was a strong scent hanging in the air. It was a familiar kind of funny smell – but what was it?

Suddenly, there was a loud snarl. *'Groggggh!'*

They had heard this noise so many times in battle before that instantly they knew what it was. It was a cry of 'charge!' that the Rochgwars sometimes used. This one came from a Rochgwar who didn't like his shoulders patted. The two Guardians turned and fled. They remembered to take their blindfolds off before running, though.

'Something beginning with "R"!' a voice echoed down the tunnel as it retreated.

Chapter Twenty-One
Evasive Action

'Why is it so bright here?' asked Cut in the third tunnel. 'I thought Rochgwar tunnels were dark, depressing places.'

'There are torches about every five hundred paces, I estimate. This must be an important tunnel,' explained Ember, who happened to be a Master Shot. Before he started on his training, Ember was mentored by his dad. But something dreadful happened. His dad was wounded in battle and could not carry on. His last words were, 'Become a Master Shot, lad, it's glorious!' Ember decided to fulfil his dad's last words. Before long, he started training. He found the bow harder that he expected, but he soon became good at hitting targets from afar, like his father had. His other skills were sharpening arrows and sword fighting. He was known among the senior Guardians to be trustworthy, dependable, and rule-abiding, which is why on this mission he was third in command, after Slick and Robin.

'What's this?' asked Cut, obviously surprised. 'An obstacle course? A challenge? A test?' He pointed at what lay ahead.

'All three,' Ember replied.

The obstacle course looked very dangerous. It had spikes you had to leap over and hammers mashing together. It was manned by a group of injured Rochgwars who had expected to have a quiet day, but who had now detected the two Guardians and were shooting arrows, waving spears and roaring out loud at them.

'This shouldn't be too hard,' said Cut, just before he was whacked by a stone thrown by a Rochgwar.

Ember sighed. 'Why was I picked to go with this idiot?' he wondered. 'Right!' he snapped. 'Put your shield in front of you, and on the count of three, jump over the spikes!' Cut did as he was told.

'One, two, three!' yelled Ember. They did a leap, over the spikes, somersaulted and landed on some rocky ground.

'Now,' said Ember, 'for the hammers!'

'How will we get through?' wailed Cut.

Just then, a Rochgwar charged at them from behind the hammers. It obviously thought it could pass through the deadly mallets, but it was wrong. *Smash!* The monster was broken up and the machine jammed before it broke up in a cloud of dust.

'Oh well,' said Ember. 'I guess that's sorted then.' But they didn't have time to utter a word of celebration, because arrows were raining down on them!

'Take cover!' shouted Cut. Ember didn't listen. He rolled forward three times and slammed into a Rochgwar, then slashed two others with his sword, shoved another one against the wall with his shield, then kicked yet another Rochgwar slap bang backwards into a sixth.

'Great job, Ember!' said Cut. 'But I hope there's one for me to bash!'

'There is!' roared Ember, because a Rochgwar had thrown him to the ground and was getting ready to beat him up. Cut jumped into the air, grabbed a torch and hurled it at the Rochgwar. The Rochgwar found itself on fire and shrieked madly before it crumbled.

'I guess that's that,' said Ember.

'No, it isn't!' shouted Cut. 'Look!'

A whole group of Rochgwars was charging towards them.

Chapter Twenty-Two
The Capture and the Rescue

The four Guardians who had made it out of the first two tunnels and back into the clearing were anxious about how long they should wait for the others. Nitro suggested something to pass the time, but the others were not so keen.

'Who says it's a rubbish game?' pressed Nitro.

'Arghhhh!' screamed Slick.

'Let's play it anyway,' said Heath. 'My turn first! I spy, with my little eye, something beginning with 'R'!'

'Rocks!' exclaimed Jack.

'Right!'

'My turn then!'

Reader, you know the rules of I-Spy. Let's just skip to the answers.

'Dirt!'

'Boulder!'

'Tunnel!'

All of a sudden, Slick interrupted them. 'I spy with my little eye, something beginning with "M"!'

'Erm ... monkey?' offered Nitro.

'No!'

'Mascot?'

'No, it's "monsters"!' said Slick just as he was overrun by the rocky figures. The other Guardians managed to pick off a few monsters but most of them were overpowered. 'Oof!' said Jack as he was thrown to the ground.

The Guardians certainly hadn't expected this attack. 'Didn't expect this, did you?' sneered the lead Rochgwar. 'I'll be promoted for this!'

The children were tied up, bundled into sacks and carried away.

'Not so bored now, are you?' said Slick to Nitro before his head disappeared into the sack.

*   *   *

Ember and Cut sat asleep. Suddenly, there was a *'Tchak!'* noise. Ember bolted upright. 'Cut!' said Ember. 'Was that you?'

114

'No!' replied Cut. Then again ... *thunk!*

'Stop it, Cut!' Ember tried to move but his hands were tied behind his back. He also seemed to have been tied to Cut.

'It's not me!'

After a short pause ... *tack! Tich!*

'See?' said Cut. 'It's not me.'

'*Psst!* You lot! Over here!' came a voice from behind some stones.

'Talking stones!' gasped Cut.

'No, it's us!' hissed the voice. Crouched down, keeping a low profile, were Robin and Fil.

'How did you get in?' asked Cut.

'Well,' explained Robin, 'our tunnel led us here. There may be four entrances on the side we came, but I don't think here are four exits on the other side. Some of the tunnels must link together.'

'We had nothing to biff along the way. How irritating is that?' Fil complained.

None of the words made any real sense to the captured Guardians.

Ember and Cut heard a whistling sound as a blade sliced through the air, and suddenly they could move their hands.

'Thanks for freeing us, Robin,' they said with much gratitude. 'And ahem …' prompted Fil.

'Oops, and you too, Cabinet Guardian.' Cabinet Guardian was their nickname for Fil. (Remember that his name is pronounced 'File'? Like 'filing cabinet'.)

116

Of course, he didn't like it.

'Thanks,' he said sarcastically.

'Have you seen Nitro, Slick, Heath and Jack?' asked Robin.

'I've just been bound next to Ember all this time in this dark cave,' whinged Cut. 'There's nothing to see.'

'Let's go back to the clearing,' said Fil.

'Not back again through this tunnel though!' shrieked Ember.

'I second that!' shouted Cut.

'Alright. Alright! We'll go back through the tunnel Fil and I came from,' Robin decided. 'Even though this tunnel here carries on further, I think we should walk back to the clearing first, link up with the others, and then check out the other two tunnels. I suspect one of them takes us where we want to eventually be.' They quietly trudged back down the fourth tunnel, where Robin and Fil had come from, towards the clearing.

Chapter Twenty-Three
No Way Out

In the Rochgwar camp, morning was breaking. Grunted had been in a very good mood the previous evening. He had been informed by two Rochgwar guards that two junior Guardians had been captured in one of the tunnels. They had been left there overnight, so he rose slowly and decided to bring them in himself for questioning.

It was a long walk down the dark tunnels, but Grunted was in a cheerful mood, happily chatting with the two Rochgwar guards accompanying him. The three arrived at the spot where Ember and Cut had been left behind.

'Where! Have! They! Gone?' shrieked Grunted.

'Wotisit, sir, wotisit?' said one of the Rochgwars, trying to be helpful.

'Can't! You! See?' shouted Grunted. 'The two prisoners have escaped! Why was no one left to guard them!'

'Well, sir, er ... the two prisoners had been bound hand and foot ... er ... they couldn't have moved, and ... er ...'

'Well, where are they now? All the other tunnels link to this one, and this one exits to our camp. We've just come from the other end. They could be in our camp by now, which obviously has not happened, or we would have met them along the way. They could either be further down this one, or they could have gone into any of the other three.

'I'm not hunting around all the other tunnels because you two weren't smart enough to keep the two captured prisoners captured. *Epso grundtinun!* That's three days of rock digging punishment for you!' fumed Grunted as he spun around to make the long walk out of the tunnel.

*   *   *

'It seems quiet around here,' said Cut, as they walked down the fourth, empty tunnel. Compared to the third, where he and Ember had dodged a whole obstacle course, and fought against Rochgwars, this one seemed like a stroll in the park.

'Don't tempt fate,' warned Ember. 'Be careful what you wish for.'

'Stop being so negative, Ember. Relax a bit. Where's your sense of adventure? Where's your sense of fun?'

'I am adventurous and fun,' Ember protested. Fil and Cut burst out laughing. Even Robin had to hold back a smile.

'You? You are the most cautious junior Guardian I know!' Fil laughed.

'Yes, but …' Ember stopped talking as the faint sound of singing could be heard from the end of the tunnel. They paused briefly to listen, and there was only one thing it could be. Rochgwars were coming from the other end of the fourth tunnel, returning from the fight at Delton.

'Should we go back the way we came?' asked Cut.

'Let's just head back to where we rescued you,' Robin said. 'We'll turn left where this tunnel joins, closer towards the obstacle course you went through. They are probably turning right and moving back to their camp. We'll hide there for a while.'

'But what if we –' Cut protested, but was quickly bundled along.

'Come on! Quick!' Robin ordered.

They hurried along back the way they came. Robin and Fil had now walked back and forth over the same stretch of the tunnel three times. Where the fourth tunnel linked to the third, they turned left and carried on for about a hundred paces, a bit beyond where they had found Ember and Cut, and hid and waited. A terrible song soon cut through the air, raking their ear drums. It started from tiny whispers and got louder and louder. The Guardians waited for what seemed like forever. The noise of the singing, combined with the echoes down the walls of the tunnel, made them slightly dizzy.

The walls of the base
Go down and down
Down and down
Down and down ...

'Here they come! Don't move!' ordered Robin as the Rochgwars came into view, turned right and moved in the opposite direction. This was a very large group, and the line of marching Rochgwars seemed to go on forever. Some of the Rochgwars looking to be tossing sacks amongst themselves, like beach balls. The Guardians counted four of them. *'Mrggh! Mrggh!'* said a wriggling sack.

123

The last row of Rochgwars finally went past, and when Robin sneaked ahead to confirm all was clear, and that there were no more Rochgwars trailing behind, the Guardians had a quick discussion.

'I think we should follow them,' said Cut.

'I agree,' said Robin.

'But what about the others? They might have hidden out of sight, and let these silly monsters past ... they might still be waiting for us at the clearing,' Ember warned. 'We can't leave them there waiting.'

The Rochgwars' songs continued to echo down the tunnel, in time to their footsteps, although the singing grew fainter.

Robin considered that the others might still be waiting at the clearing. There was the chance, of course, that they had hidden out of sight as the Rochgwars passed by. But it was strangely coincidental that the Rochgwars were in a jolly mood, carrying four sacks. And as the leader of this unit, he had to make a decision.

'We will follow them,' he decided. Sometimes leaders had to make difficult decisions.

Chapter Twenty-Four
Deeper in Trouble

The Rochgwars were still singing the same song, in time to their marching. They had just got to the verse that goes:

The Guardians in the base go
'Wah! Wah! Wah!'
'Wah! Wah! Wah!'

Said one Rochgwar at the rear to another, 'This is my favourite song. I really …'

Paff! Something whacked into him. 'You really what?' asked the other, before he was hit by Fil and crumbled beside his comrade. Fil and Cut were about to race ahead and start clubbing more Rochgwars but Robin and Ember held them back.

'Shhh! Not too fast! A few at a time! That way they don't notice!' hissed Robin.

'Oh, all right then,' grumbled Fil.

'The leaders in the base go *Weep! Weep! Weep!*' sang a Rochgwar. Suddenly – *wham!* An arrow lodged itself right in his back and he never made it to the next verse.

And so the junior Guardians kept repeating this manoeuvre, slowly attacking the Rochgwars from the rear and picking them off one at a time. The few Rochgwars that did notice the Guardians striking them from the back were attacked rapidly and crumbled. Even those that let out a cry of pain or warning found their voices lost in the singing of the Rochgwars. The Guardians thought that their plan was going very well, apart from Fil who was getting bored and annoyed that he couldn't just bash everything in sight but had to do it bit by bit. It was like trying to eat a big meal using toothpicks.

127

Suddenly, two arrows whizzed through the air and hit Rochgwars carrying a sack. The Rochgwars crumbled and the sack fell to the floor. Ember waited for a moment before rushing forward and cutting the cord with his knife. A familiar face popped out.

'Nitro?' asked Cut.

'Yes!' complained Nitro. 'Finally. Could we play *I-Spy*?'

Robin was relieved! He was never happier to see Nitro. It was not because I-Spy was his favourite game though.

There was no time for an explanation but Robin just wanted to check. 'Were you all captured?'

'Yes, and ...' but Robin put a hand up to say that explanations could wait. Ember quickly removed the cords around Nitro's wrists and ankles.

The five Guardians continued to follow the singing Rochgwars from a distance. They darted forward and back and attacked quickly, choosing to thump the Rochgwars when the volume of the singing rose. The sound echoed off the walls and still made enough noise for them not to notice anything amiss.

Nitro was relentless in attack. 'Something beginning with 'R'!' he quietly uttered each time before he smashed a Rochgwar into smaller pieces.

They marched for what seemed like an hour and the mouth of the tunnel could be seen in the distance. It began as a small circle of light that gradually increased in size as the Guardians followed behind. 'We need a plan for this!' Robin thought. But he could not give up the chance to smash Rochgwars by stopping to think. 'We'll just have to work it out when we get there,' he decided.

'Something beginning with ... R!' Nitro smashed.

'Something beginning with ... R!' Nitro smashed again.

'Something beginning with ...' Nitro stopped.

The Rochgwars had stopped marching.

Chapter Twenty-Five
Gravelburn's Great Plan

Gravelburn had turned around and was now addressing his troops. The last four or five rows of Rochgwars were still inside the tunnel, and so it looked to Gravelburn as if he still had his complete army.

'Why has he stopped to talk to us when we are still inside the tunnel?' one Rochgwar at the rear asked another.

'No one knows, but he is the leader. Do you want to ask?' replied another.

'Don't bother. You know what the answer is going to be.' *'Gravelburn is always one step ahead!'* a third mimicked in their leader's voice.

The junior Guardians could see a bit of what was going on from inside the tunnel, but were hidden from view.

'Four full moons ago, we had a plan!' Gravelburn announced, taking his time between sentences. 'We would eliminate every Guardian in Delton. And I am absolutely delighted to tell you – things are going according to the Great Plan.

'We have attacked Delton and left the Guardians in a weaker state. Why, today when we returned from the battle today, we even caught four junior Guardians. Do you know why that will be useful?' None of the assembled Rochgwars answered.

'Gravelburn is always ... one step ahead! If we need to, we will use them as hostages to force the Guardians to give up! Surely they would not sacrifice four of their younglings and forsake them!

'But we may not even need those four babies. Delton is running out of weapons and food. And soon we will take over, and use it as a base to attack other Guardian bases. We will rule the world, and these humans will become our slaves! *Graaaagh!'* He punched the air triumphantly.

'Graaaagh!' the Rochgwars echoed menacingly. They all chanted, 'All hail Gravelburn! All hail Gravelburn! One step ahead! One step ahead!'

'Idiot!' shouted Nitro between the cries. He was immediately hushed by the other Guardians. Luckily, from the back, and inside the tunnel, he could not be heard over the chanting of the Rochgwars.

Gravelburn motioned for silence. When the cheering died down, a brave Rochgwar piped up. 'But sir! We keep fighting the Guardians and losing. How can it be that we will take over their base?'

Gravelburn looked to see who had asked that question. Then he roared, 'Gravelburn is always one step ahead!'

The crowd cheered.

'We are all Rochgwars!' the leader continued. 'We –'

'I'm not,' said John, who had suddenly appeared.

There was a silence amongst the Rochgwars as they turned to see who had dared contradict their leader.

From within the tunnel, Slick whispered, 'It sounded like John.'

'John? He's still alive?' puzzled Robin.

'Quiet, you useless fleshling. Weak and traitorous, like your father.' Gravelburn could see that his words had an effect on John. The latter's fists were clenched tightly.

'Many solstices ago, the Guardians tried to blow up our base. They sent thousands of men,' Gravelburn exaggerated, 'and moved explosives through our tunnels. But I was ... one step ahead! I let them move it far enough into the tunnels, then I got one of them to work for me and lead the others into my trap. Who would have thought that, solstices later, I would come face to face with the son of Lib Rawf? Like father, like son. *Argghahahaha*!'

'Graaagh!' the Rochgwars roared.

'We now have an enormous stockpile of explosives in two of our tunnels. A massive pile. On the way back from the battle, I sent Gargna and some of the Flygwars to move them out. We are soon going to use them on Delton. I've told you before – Gravelburn is always ... one step ahead!'

'Graaaghahahaha!' the Rochgwars chorused again.

Gravelburn carried on. 'But we may not even need the explosives. We may even take down Delton without them!

'Formed from rock we are. When we get smashed into pieces, the big pieces respawn themselves into Rochgwars. The more we fall, the more Rochgwars there are!'

'Graaaghahahahahahahaha!' the Rochgwars roared.

'Now tell me – if you don't think that Gravelburn is always ... one step ahead! We have attacked Delton and the Guardians think they have defeated us. But what is there within the base now? And what is there outside the base? The Guardians think it is a whole load of defeated Rochgwars that they took down. But actually, it is hundreds and thousands of Rochgwars that will respawn! Don't think for a moment we have lost Rochgwars. We have merely created more troops for the future. The Guardians can't see it coming! And soon, Delton will be overwhelmed – completely overwhelmed – by thousands of Rochgwars. I told you Gravelburn is always ... one step ahead!'

'Oh no!' wailed Cut in a hysterical voice.

Cheers and praises rose from the crowd, and some of them high-fived themselves a bit too hard into smaller pieces, but while the warriors were distracted, Gravelburn turned around and whispered to himself, 'But when we have taken control, I will smash all the officers into little pieces and then I will be the only one in charge!'

The junior Guardians were horrified. Gravelburn's Great Plan was starting to make sense now. This was why he had been sending Rochgwars to attack Delton, even though the Rochgwars always lost. He was merely using the Guardians to break up his Rochgwars for him, and one day the broken pieces would form back into more Rochgwars to battle against the Guardians. From inside and outside the base! They had never heard of a more sinister plot. And if all that didn't work, he would just use explosives – their own weapons – against them. He truly was one step ahead.

'Can you believe he's doing this? We've been tricked all this time!' said Nitro.

'I can't believe it!' said Fil.

'Me neither,' said Ember. 'Delton will be destroyed!'

'What will we do?' wailed Cut in a hysterical voice.

'Well,' Robin said, 'maybe for starters you should all quieten down. The Rochgwars are not pleased, judging from the way they are looking at us.'

The Rochgwars had all turned around to see who was making the whimpering sounds and found themselves staring at the Guardians. The look on the faces of the stone monsters was one of puzzlement. It was as if they thought some Rochgwars had changed form into humans, and were struggling to work out how that had happened. Then the Rochgwars looked at each other blankly. And before long the blank stares hardened into grim frowns.

'I think we've spotted Guardians, haven't we?' said one Rochgwar to another.

'Yes we have, you idiot!' said his counterpart. 'Charge!'

Chapter Twenty-Six
Fighting Their Way Out

The fight ensued.

The Rochgwars and a small group of Flygwars moved to attack. But the Guardians were inside the tunnel, which meant they could stop themselves from being surrounded and overwhelmed by the larger group of enemies. Like the earlier fight in the forest – which seemed like a long time ago now – only a few of their attackers could fight at any one time.

Cut was attacking a Flygwar and was just about to smack its head when it launched into a defensive manoeuvre and beat its wings rapidly. Cut's sword smacked into one of the Flygwar's fast-beating wings and the sword just flew right back and the handle hit him on the mouth.

'Orf!' shouted Cut as he was thrown to the ground. The Flygwar was advancing steadily on Cut, until Fil sneaked up from behind it and ... *whack*! The Flygwar crumbled to dust when it felt Fil's blow.

'Thanks, Cabinet!' said Cut with gratitude.

'Don't mention it!' said Fil, as he searched for even more monsters to do battle with. 'Finally! All that time I've been waiting for a big fight!'

Robin was battling a particularly angry Rochgwar which was putting up a good fight. Each attacked and thrusted. The other defended and blocked the blow. The fight was headed for a stalemate, until Ember joined in and the two Guardians double-teamed it.

'Evasive manoeuvres!' cried Ember as the Rochgwar swung his sword. After the miss, the Rochgwar was preparing to deliver the next blow when Robin knocked it to the ground. Then Ember smashed it to pieces.

'Thanks for the help Ember!' gasped Robin.

'That's all right,' said Ember in a monotone.

Cut and Nitro were being attacked by five Rochgwars. Nitro managed to fend one off, but both Guardians were outnumbered by the rest of the monsters. But just when a Rochgwar was about to smack Nitro (for the eleventh time), the other Shock Unit members appeared and helped out.

'Ta!' said Nitro.

But the Rochgwars just kept coming.

'More Uglies!' shouted Ember.

'Knock knock!' said Nitro.

'Look out!' shouted Fil, dodging the blow of a Flygwar.

'I've got this one!' Ember shouted, moving up to send a Rochgwar packing.

'Knock knock!' said Nitro again.

'Who's there?' answered Robin. They were in the middle of a fight but someone needed to answer, or else Nitro would just keep on going until someone did.

'Gravel!'

'Gravel who?' asked Robin.

'Gravelburn, that's who,' said Cut, finishing for Nitro.

'That's a terrible joke, and not really the right time for it,' shouted Fil to Nitro, in between bashing a Rochgwar.

'No time for arguing,' said Cut. 'Here really comes Gravelburn!'

The action stopped.

All was quiet.

Even the Rochgwars froze in mid-action. One had been ready to hit Cut – his weapon had paused right above the Guardian's head as he turned to look at the Supreme Leader. Cut seized the chance and hit the Rochgwar as hard as he could while he had the chance.

'Hey! That's not fair,' the piece that used to be the head said before the face dimmed and disappeared.

The stone warriors parted. Someone dark, someone vicious, someone who didn't know the meaning of fear – only violence – stepped forward towards the Guardians.

'Well then, so this is the invincible Shock Unit that managed to hold out against my warriors' force and power,' said Gravelburn.

'Never mind that!' growled Ember. 'Give us back our friends!'

'You mean these three useless bundles?' sneered Gravelburn. He waved his hand dismissively and Rochgwars threw down three sacks which Gravelburn kicked forward. Robin, Nitro and Cut slashed open the sacks. Inside were Slick, Jack and Heath.

'Take back your friends. Useless things. They don't matter any more,' said Gravelburn. 'You're all going to be eliminated anyway! The whole of Delton is probably waking up to thousands of Rochgwars tomorrow. And everyone is invited to the fireworks show!'

Chapter Twenty-Seven
Rebellion in the Ranks

'How are you three?' asked Fil.

'Dazed.'

'Tired from being bounced around!'

'Nearly deaf because of the terrible singing!'

'Hey!' protested a Rochgwar. 'I don't think we sing that badly, do we?'

'If you think we're bad,' said another, 'listen to Gravelburn! He sings like a mouse with a sore throat that's being stepped on by an elephant!'

Gravelburn seemed hurt by this remark and punched the Rochgwar nearest to him to pieces.

'As I was saying,' said Gravelburn, 'before my beautiful singing received such great comments, I don't need you any more, now that my Great Plan is in action. It was supposed to be a secret and I've accidentally told you about it, but you're too late to stop it anyway.

'Phases one and two are already being put into action. Isn't that right, my faithful army?'

But the stone monsters were now actually too busy arguing about whose singing was better, than to listen to their leader.

'My singing is a hundred per cent better than yours!' said one warrior to another.

'Oh yeah? Mine is ten million per cent better than yours!'

'You see my fist, don't you? Want to look at it real close?'

'Guys! Guys! Guys!' a Rochgwar shouted, and waited for everyone to quieten down before continuing. 'Guys! Let's agree on something – Gravelburn's singing is the worst.'

'Yes!' came a whole chorus of replies.

'He has the voice of a trampled pig!' a voice piped up, and some Rochgwars laughed at this comment.

'When he marches with us, he never sings in time!' More laughs and nods.

'And that's because Gravelburn …'

'… is always one step ahead!'

The laughs were spreading throughout the Rochgwar army. The Rochgwars had lived under Gravelburn's rule for so long, and were so fed up about it, they were now seizing the chance to mock him.

'He doesn't even know the words to "The walls of the base"!'

'Once I was near him, and heard him sing, *"The walls of the base go ploop ploop ploop!"*' another Rochgwar revealed.

The battleground was now just a circus of laughs. Even Ember was cracking a smile.

'Alright, that's it now,' fumed Gravelburn and dived right into the laughing Rochgwars and starting throwing punches. Soon it was every Rochgwar for himself. They fought and the skirmish spilled over to outside the tunnel.

The Guardians stepped out into the open to a chaotic scene of stone warriors biffing each other up. John could not be seen anywhere. But now that their enemies were fighting amongst themselves, this was their chance to regroup.

'So, Robin, how do we move on to the next stage of our plan?' asked Jack. 'Do we send a messenger owl?'

'I would send a messenger owl, because I love owls, but there's just one problem,' said Robin. 'We don't have any owls because we were in a cave! I mean, there are some birds that live in caves, but it would take too long to find one!'

Suddenly, an eagle let out a piercing cry from overhead. 'I'd recognise that cry anywhere!' shouted Slick. 'Hunter! Hunter! Over here!' He started acting like a squirrel and the eagle, its attention drawn, circled around. When it recognised a familiar face it descended onto Slick's outstretched arm.

'Good boy!' said Slick, petting the eagle's head. 'I lost him a while ago. I sent him away and he never came back. Oh, it's so good to see you, Hunter!'

They quickly hurried out of sight because Ember had spotted something coming out from the tunnel.

Suddenly, Gargna emerged, slightly unsure of what was going on. There just appeared to be lots of fighting among Rochgwars.

'Boss!' he shouted out. 'Boss!'

'What is it, Gargna?' came the infuriated reply. 'Can't you see I'm busy?' said Gravelburn in between punches and jabs.

'We located the boxes of explosives in the tunnels. But there were too many and too heavy for us to shift, so I've marked their position and we can all go and move them out tomorrow.'

'Good job, Gargna!' cried Gravelburn. He turned around to thump another Rochgwar. 'Good job!'

Grunted had now appeared next to Gargna. 'You "marked them out",' he said, doing the inverted comma action with his fingers. 'But with what?'

'Well, it's all dark in the tunnels, and I don't want to forget where they were, like I heard you did with some prisoners that you captured ...' Gargna paused to see Grunted's reaction to the insult.

'... so I put torches on the edges of some boxes, and when we're walking down the tunnels tomorrow we can easily locate what we want.'

'You marked their position with torches?' Grunted said incredulously. 'Rocks for brains, what happens when the torches burn down?'

The fighting of Rochgwar against Rochgwar was suddenly interrupted by an earth-shattering explosion. There was a huge boom and the ground shook fearfully. This was echoed by other explosions split seconds later, as box after box of explosives ignited from within the tunnels. Stones rained down from the sky. Everyone crouched and huddled, and when they looked up after the ground had stopped vibrating and debris was no longer falling from the sky, Rochg Infini seemed to have lost its right shoulder.

'Er …' stammered Gargna. 'Like I said, there was quite a lot, too much for us to move …'

'Epso ritor igranus vush apta nor sher grata! Grupa grundi rodh im epsun, dor vush ranta mei - epsin gratanei!' roared Gravelburn. Things were definitely NOT going to plan.

John suddenly appeared beside Gravelburn. 'This old Rochgwarian language you speak sounds so beautiful. I would really like to learn it. Can you teach me?'

Seething with fury, Gravelburn clonked John on the head, nearly knocking him out cold.

(Reader, I bet you can guess what happened next. You're right!) John recovered and clonked Gravelburn on the head - definitely not a good idea.

153

So Gravelburn did his signature kick on John's femur. Since Gravelburn was part stone, his kick felt as painful as a boulder on your little toe. John screamed so loudly that a nearby Rochgwar shattered into pieces.

John carried on and kicked Gravelburn in the thigh. This again was not a good idea. Number one: it makes Gravelburn angry. Number two: you will hurt your foot kicking stone. John hopped around like mad holding his foot. This trading of blows was going nowhere, and so to end the fight, the stone warriors thumped both on their heads, knocking them out cold.

While all this was going on, the Guardians were writing a message in code and it looked something like this:

It meant: *Beware! The enemy is leading you into a trap!*
Break up every big rock in and around Delton to defend it!

Chapter Twenty-Eight
Training Pays Off

Hunter the eagle took off at the time John kicked Gravelburn.
But John and Gravelburn were not the only two fighting.
Immediately after the junior Guardians sent the message,
they were faced with angry warriors swarming with hatred.
The stone warriors advanced, hurling rocks as they charged.
Flygwars swooped above the Guardians, dive-bombing them.
To the children, it seemed like this was it. Never again would
they return to Delton. Never again would they get to lie in
their nice log beds. Instead they would spend the rest of their
lives being servants to these cold rock monsters. The
thought filled them with fear. But Robin refused to give up or
give in.

'Group together! Raise your shields over your head!' he
commanded. 'This way it will protect against these flying
things!'

Robin was right. The Flygwars just slammed into the Shock Unit shields every time they dived. They might have been partly made from rock, but they had their limits. After about eleven tries, they gave up and retreated to rest their aching heads.

They had got rid of one threat, but the Rochgwars were still in the fight. Actually, the Rochgwars were fighting among themselves as much as against the Guardians.

'Right!' shouted Robin. 'Now turn your shields at a seventy-degree angle to defend against these stones they're throwing at us!' And with that all-round protection, Robin led Shock Unit in their march forward.

(Before you read this part, do you know of the Roman formation, the tortoise? What the Guardians did was a bit like it. Imagine you're outside. You point your finger at the sun. Your finger is the shield. Well, sorry I can't explain it any better. Alright! Back to the chapter!)

The shields protected the Guardians from rocks coming from all directions. Each time a rock hit a Guardian shield, it just bounced off, although shields dented and cracked a little. Rochgwars that did come close enough were clubbed or speared from under the metallic protection.

'I don't think my shield can hold out much longer!' said Jack. He was at the right side of the formation.

'Mine neither!' said Cut on the left.

Suddenly, there was a loud thump and Jack's shield just broke into two pieces!

Jack looked left. Jack looked right.

Jack saw Rochgwars charging towards him. They had spotted the defensive gap in the formation. And they knew that there was a weak spot they could take advantage of. In that split second, as Jack looked down at what had been his

158

shield and up at the Rochgwars, he knew what they were thinking. His heart had been thumping as he fought, but now it beat even faster. The Rochgwars charged. Jack yelled. The Guardians on either side of him swivelled their shields around to cover for him as he retreated into the circle for protection. Everyone braced themselves for impact, especially Robin, who was directly in line with the oncoming Rochgwars.

The stone warriors charged as the shields closed around, and spears, swords and clubs appeared from under the circular wall of metal. The Rochgwars had charged so fast that they couldn't stop, and slammed into Shock Unit. Fragments of stone flew everywhere! Robin was a bit shaken up but was still fine. And on the far side, Ember and Cut, now led the Guardians next to them from opposite directions, pivoting around Robin so Shock Unit now formed a new circle, facing inwards, around the one or two surviving Rochgwars. The Rochgwars were trapped and finished off easily. It was the classic Guardian 'pivot-and-pincer' movement they had practised so many times in training.

The Guardians then swivelled their shields outward again for protection from the next wave of attacks. They made sure to keep Jack in their middle of their formation so he was always protected, but he had now picked up two clubs and could defend himself from approaching Rochgwars, or get at them when they were enclosed. Shock Unit held firm, repeating their tactical movement again and again.

Suddenly, after beating off another Rochgwar attack, a sword struck Robin out of nowhere as he turned his shield outwards, and he felt to the ground, stunned. John's sword was raised high above his head. But as John considered his next move, Robin picked up a rock – there was plenty to choose from – and launched it in John's direction. It hit him directly in the face. John's head jerked backwards and he fell to the ground, not moving.

Now only Gravelburn and his two Rochgwar guards stood on the battlefield.

'Ahem.' Gravelburn cleared his throat and stuttered, as the Guardians took out the guards, to leave him as the only one standing. 'I've been doing some thinking and wondered perhaps if we could come to some sort of arrangement?'

Chapter Twenty-Nine
The Capture

'No!' said Robin sternly. 'We can't just come to "some arrangement"!'

'Yeah!' echoed Slick, raising his sword and waving it threateningly.

Ember moved forward and said calmly, 'You've done enough, Gravelburn. It's time to face justice.'

Cut, who by this time was just going around breaking bigger pieces of rock into smaller ones, turned around and said, 'I don't know what you said, but I'm with you!'

They had cornered Gravelburn but he was going to take his chances against eight children if he could not blag his way out of it. Eight on one. Not a very good situation to be in. But as Gravelburn stared at the children, and as they hesitated, he made a break for the tunnel. The Guardians gave chase. As Gravelburn looked to make his escape, there was a lot of noise and dust coming from inside the tunnel, and a group of Guardians emerged with two carts! They easily pinned the Rochgwar leader to the ground.

An officer jumped off. 'Lieutenant Vei Sirage of Delton at your service, Sir!' He barked and saluted Robin.

'Why are you saluting me?' asked Robin, confused. 'You're higher in rank than I am.'

'Not any more,' replied Vei Sirage, 'since you have been promoted to Captain.' Robin's heart skipped a beat. A Captain on his ninth birthday!

'The others are also promoted to commanders,' continued Vei Sirage as his men tied Gravelburn up. 'Murx Espin's orders. They will lead their own units now. Ember will lead

Stealth Unit, Heath will be in charge of Messenger Unit, and Slick will command Attack Unit.

'Nitro is in charge of Creation Unit; Jack, Blacksmith Unit; Cut, Swift Unit; and Fil, Sharp Unit. But when trouble brews, you will all be called together to help defend Delton and fight off its enemies.

'And one last thing.'

'Yes?' asked Robin.

'Murx Espin has decided to change Shock Unit's name to Power Unit – that is what you will all be called when you are together.' The Power Unit commanders' first act was to give Gravelburn a good kick.

'Not too hard!' cautioned Ember. 'We don't want him breaking off into mini Gravelburns!'

164

'Sir!' continued Vei Sirage. 'We have a transport for you and the other commanders to ride back in.' He pointed to the other cart and motioned for them to climb aboard.

'I'm thinking of changing my new unit's name already,' thought Heath. 'I'll ask Murx Espin if I can call it ' "Whenever",' he muttered.

'You want to call it "Whenever"?' puzzled Slick.

'Yes, that's right. I'll be there Whenever Unit me,' he said to a chorus of laughs.

'Hey, Robin!' asked Ember. 'Do you know what happened to John?' The other Guardians had not seen Robin defend himself from John, and had no idea of John's condition.

'Mmrgh?' said Robin blankly as he sat down. Robin was thinking about the ghost he saw in the tunnel. He was thinking about quite a lot of other things too, and there were a lot of unanswered questions in his mind.

'So many unanswered questions ...' he said drowsily. *'And not enough answers,'* a voice in his head replied. Robin froze. He knew that voice. Was it ...

'John?' said Robin in a small voice.

'Yes, John,' said Ember, who had sat down next to him. 'What happened to him?'

So Robin explained what had happened on the ride back to Delton. They both decided they could tell the others at a later time.

When they arrived, a feast was awaiting them. Some tables had been set up and food had been laid out. There was chicken, boar, wild pig, wine, humbugs, cake and pudding in the Great Hall. Jolly music filled the air. Robin shut his eyes and took in the beautiful scents of the food. It was a mix of lovely smells and he could not wait to tuck in. When he opened his eyes, he noticed that for some reason the Cabinet Guardian Fil was now conducting the orchestra.

'Who would have thought that Fil was so musical!' chuckled Ember.

'Yer!' said Slick. (It means 'yes', just very heavily-accented.) 'I'm just thinking about him playing the clarinet!'

'Haha!' Robin laughed as he chomped into a chicken drumstick. Fil would rather use a clarinet to hit a Rochgwar than play it. 'Mmmmm! This food is good!'

'Yes!' said a server. 'It should be! The food is from around the base. Locally-sourced food. Local specialities should taste good, Captain Robin.'

The music played on as the laughter flowed as freely as the food and drink. The feast went on even as the moon hung high in the dark sky. And in the tunnels, pieces of rock littered the floor, a reminder of the Guardian victory.

And then some rocks began to vibrate.

Epilogue

Gravelburn was kept in prison for forty days and nights before he mysteriously disappeared. It was thought that he had escaped to the eastern border because there were unconfirmed sightings of him there. This is the story most Guardians believe happened.

* * *

Gravelburn sat in his cell, feeling very, very bored. The cell was in the far corner of the camp, opposite the gates, at the foot of one of the watchtowers. He was tired of being asked to play 'I-Spy' by Nitro, who came round quite often.

'I wish someone would rescue me,' thought Gravelburn. 'Any time would be great.'

'Cell!' shouted Nitro. 'Cell begins with "C"! My turn again until you get it right!'

Suddenly, a stone hit Gravelburn on the head. There was something tied around it. A note! This is what it said:

Gravelburn, we shall break you out in five days' time when the dumb guard Flick comes on duty. When he arrives, throw this stone and note over the walls. It will be a signal to us.

With love (NOT!),
John

And so it was planned. But first – 'Cell again! Come on, make a guess! You've got to try!' - more days of 'I-Spy'.

*   *   *

'I really have a bad job,' thought Flick five days later. He hated being on sentry duty and was engrossed in his thoughts of misery. He didn't understand why Gravelburn was so happy to see him, and he also didn't see Gravelburn chuck a rock over the perimeter walls. Moments later there was an explosion, one that threw Flick to the ground and leaving him temporarily stunned. Something hovered over the perimeter walls.

'Hello again, Gravelburn,' boomed the ghost of John, as the door to the cell fell off its hinges.

'Quick!' said John. 'We won't have much time before he wakes up or the others come!' So Gravelburn climbed over the perimeter walls while John floated over, both determined to wreck havoc on Delton again when the time was right ...

Printed in Great Britain
by Amazon

37427058R00099